The Magic Rug of Grand-Pré

Réjean Aucoin and Jean-Claude Tremblay
Illustrations: Herménégilde Chiasson
Translation: Barbara LeBlanc and Sally Ross

NIMBUS PUBLISHING LIMITED

It was Christmas Eve in Chéticamp. Everybody in the village was getting ready for the festivities. Like all the other children on Cape Breton Island, the twins Rose-Marie and Constant tingled with excitement at the sight of all the activity around them. In a few hours, they would be attending Midnight Mass for the first time. When they got back, there would be a wonderful supper and lots of surprises under the Christmas tree.

Even though they were twins, they didn't look alike. Constant was as round as a barrel, and Rose-Marie was as slender as a string bean.

Unable to sit still, Rose-Marie and Constant began racing all over the house. They were getting in everyone's way and making it impossible for their mother, their sisters, and their aunts to finish preparing the Christmas Eve supper.

Grannie Henriette was tired of watching them run around. She pulled her rocking chair over beside the woodstove and said, "Come sit on my knee. Let me tell you a story before you go to bed. See the rug on the wall? A long, long time ago, my great-great-grandmother hooked that rug with some of her friends. Do you recognize anything?"

"Yes, Grannie," said Rose-Marie, "it's the church in Grand-Pré."

"But why is there some wool missing from the top of the steeple?" asked Constant, as curious as a cat.

Nestled in Grannie Henriette's arms, the two children listened as she began to tell the story of the hooked rug from Grand-Pré.

"It is a very old hooked rug, and as Constant noticed, it was never finished and probably never will be. My great-great-grandmother and her friends didn't have time to hook the cross on the steeple. They started the rug in 1755, the year the Acadians were deported. The women in Grand-Pré had decided to hook a rug for their parish. It was to be hung behind the main altar of the church for all the parishioners to proudly admire. But there was no Christmas in Grand-Pré that year. The British soldiers arrived . . . and the Acadians were loaded onto ships and transported far and wide. That is why the rug was never completed.

"During those years of hardship, my great-great-grandmother was a little luckier than the others. She and her family managed to escape the Deportation. During their flight northward, the rug protected them from the snow of winter, the wind of autumn, the rain of spring, and the heat of summer. Ever since then, it has been kept in this very house in Chéticamp, and we have been the guardians of the rug."

Grannie Henriette paused for a moment, lost in her memories. A stillness descended over the house. The children waited attentively. Even the women had stopped working to listen to the story about the rug from Grand-Pré.

"If only we could find the twelve missing strands of wool to finish the rug," Grannie Henriette added wistfully.

Rose-Marie and Constant stared at the rug in amazement. Their eyes were drawn to the empty spot on the top of the steeple. Suddenly, the twelve missing strands of wool became very important. They had disappeared with Grannie Henriette's ancestors, and for some mysterious reason, the rug could only be finished if those strands were found. Without the twelve strands of wool, the cross on the steeple would remain empty forever.

"Oh, how happy I would be if the missing strands could be found. It would be the happiest Christmas of my life," exclaimed Grannie Henriette.

The children let their imaginations wander as they gazed at the rug. The women went back to work. They still had many meat pies and apple pies to make for the friends and relatives invited to the supper after

Midnight Mass. The entire household purred happily while the chicken fricot bubbled on the stove, sending out its wonderful aroma.

It was about seven-thirty when the Mailman, Johnny à Minou, knocked at the door. The villagers were convinced that there was something magic about his long legs. Johnny à Minou delivered the mail all over the Chéticamp area, from La Prairie down to Belle

Côte. Three times a week he travelled forty miles on foot to Inverness to pick up the mail.

"Merry Christmas to you all!" he called out as he closed the door behind him. "I think I have time to get warmed up. A little drink would do me a world of good, Henriette. It's cold out there."

"Come on in. I'll give you something to loosen up your tongue, and you can tell us the latest news from the village."

Without having to be coaxed, Johnny à Minou pulled up a chair. He noticed the twins staring at the rug. Their eyes were fixed on the empty spot on top of the church steeple. Turning to Henriette, Johnny à Minou said, "What's the matter with those two? They're pretty quiet tonight."

"Don't worry, Johnny, it's the story of the rug that calmed them down, the same story that made you daydream when you were their age."

"You're curious about Grannie Henriette's rug, eh?" asked Johnny à Minou.

"Maybe if we looked around in the attic, we'd find the twelve missing strands of wool," said Constant.

"I doubt it," replied Johnny à Minou. "During the Deportation, men, women, and children and those

twelve strands were scattered in all directions. But don't give up hope. Someday we'll find the twelve strands and then . . ."

"Then what?" asked Rose-Marie.

"Then we'll enter the magical world of our ancestors—"

"Don't start putting ideas into their heads," interrupted Grannie Henriette. "I know you and your stories."

Johnny à Minou winked at the twins and whispered, "You'd better go have a nap, you've got a long night ahead of you."

He kissed them good night and wished them sweet dreams. The door had hardly closed behind the children when he said, "Well, Henriette, I must be on my way. I've put your mail on the counter. I have a lot of things to do for Christmas Eve. Good night!"

Johnny à Minou disappeared like a fox into the night.

Meanwhile, Rose-Marie and Constant were so excited about the rug and the Christmas Eve celebrations that they had trouble falling asleep. It was a clear night, and the snow was falling gently on Chéticamp.

The twins had hardly warmed up the sheets when they heard a knock on the window. They recognized Johnny à Minou's voice at once.

"Constant, Rose-Marie, come to the window if you want to find the missing strands of wool and make your grandmother happy."

Who could resist an invitation like that, especially from Johnny à Minou? Certainly not Constant and Rose-Marie.

"If you promise to keep it a secret, I will help you find the twelve strands of wool," said Johnny à Minou.

The twins keep a secret? They could keep the biggest secret in the world to make Grannie Henriette happy.

"As you know, I have the reputation of being a fast runner, a really fast runner, at least that's what they say. Well, I can run even faster when it's for a good cause, especially on Christmas Eve. I can even run faster than the southeast wind that blows down from the mountains. Thanks to the wind fairies who gave me my seven-league legs, I'm a magic mailman. Go get dressed warmly, and I'll get some food. Then we'll go looking for the twelve strands of wool."

The children jumped for joy. They were ready in a flash. They put their clothes on over their pyjamas, pulled their hats down over their ears and their mittens right up to their elbows. Rose-Marie called impatiently to Constant, "Hurry up! Johnny won't wait forever!"

Meanwhile, without being seen, Johnny à Minou took the rug and one of the pies that Grannie Henriette had put on the window ledge to cool.

"Come on, children, climb into my mailbag and hold on tight."

Johnny à Minou, as excited as the twins, soon proved his legendary speed. This was the man who could leap over a fence without missing a step and who could catch a fox on the run. In a hop, skip, and a jump, he was over the church in Chéticamp and racing toward the stars with Constant and Rose-Marie.

The children, wide eyed, looked down as sleepy Cape Breton villages swept by: Plateau, Saint Joseph du Moine, and Margaree. Johnny à Minou beamed happily. Striding from one star to another, he carried the twins closer to the magical world of their ancestors.

"The only person who can help us find the missing strands of wool is Gaby, the historian on Île Madame," said Johnny à Minou. "He has all kinds of books and documents about the Deportation of our ancestors. He'll be glad to help us."

"We're really high up, Johnny," Rose-Marie said in a shivery voice. "What's the name of that great big river down there?"

"That's not a river, it's the Strait of Canso, and that means we're almost at Gaby's house. We'll make a left turn for Île Madame. Hold on tight, it's not far, and I'll have to slow down for the landing."

Like Chéticamp, Île Madame was getting ready for the birth of the Divine Child. The snow-covered villages had a festive air, with their brightly lit windows and people coming and going. Gaby's house, set back from the road at the very end of the village of Arichat, looked warm and cosy.

Rose-Marie knocked on the door. She was just about to knock a second time when the door opened a crack and an inquisitive face peeked out.

"My name is Rose-Marie, and this is my twin brother, Constant. Is this the home of Gaby the historian?"

It was as if Rose-Marie had said a password. The door opened immediately, and Gaby, whose real name was Gabriel, invited them in. Rose-Marie and Constant didn't think he looked at all like a historian. He was a young and sturdy man who stood as straight as a post and who spoke with a strong, deep voice.

"So, you're the twins. Well, show me the famous rug."

Imagine Rose-Marie's and Constant's surprise. How could Gabriel have guessed the purpose of their visit? With Johnny à Minou's help, the twins spread out Grannie Henriette's rug on the floor.

"Yes, it's definitely the rug from Grand-Pré," said Gabriel with tears in his eyes and a lump in his throat. "I know why you're here."

With that, he disappeared into the next room and came out carrying an enormous book that was almost as big as Constant. Gabriel sat down at the kitchen table and opened the precious book very carefully. Dates on the yellowed pages flew swiftly by: 1604, 1608, 1680, 1713, 1747. When he reached 1755, the year of the Deportation, Gabriel started moving his finger down the lines.

"Here it is, children. Look."

When the twins peered over Gabriel's shoulders, they were amazed to see three strands of wool marking the page.

Constant was the first to speak: "Gabriel, look at the strands of wool. I'm sure they belong to the rug from Grand-Pré."

"Wait a minute, Constant. Let's read what the book says first. It says here that the Acadians of Grand-Pré chose soft, silky wool from the best lambs in their flock. And it seems that a young shepherdess managed to save two of the lambs and take them with her when she was exiled during the Deportation.

According to this historian, the shepherdess and the two little lambs were rescued by the good Captain Beausoleil Broussard. Even the name of the shepherdess is here, or at least her first name: Thérésa. Captain Broussard took the young girl and her lambs on one of his boats and dropped them off at a place called Goose Pond."

"What about the three strands of wool?" asked Rose-Marie."Isn't there anything about the three strands?"

"Let's see," said Gabriel, "perhaps there's something a little further on. Ah! Here we are: *My mother entrusted me with three strands of wool, which I have placed in this book for safekeeping until the rug from Grand-Pré is found.* That's all it says."

Everyone in the kitchen remained silent for a long time as they thought about these precious clues. Rose-Marie asked the question that was on everyone's lips: "Where is Goose Pond?"

They all turned to Johnny à Minou, but even the Royal Mailman had to admit that he did not know. Once again, it was Rose-Marie who spoke up: "Well, if Goose Pond is shaped like a goose, then with Johnny's magic legs, perhaps we can fly high enough in the sky to recognize the pond."

"Before you go looking for the other strands, Rose-Marie, take these," said Gabriel.

The quest for the strands of wool had just taken a giant step forward, a seven-league leap. Rose-Marie very carefully picked up the three strands and placed them in the bottom-most corner of her coat pocket. She was delighted by the thought of being the guardian of a treasure.

Before the three travellers took off into the night, Gabriel went to the cupboard for an armload of provisions. He gave them some spruce beer and some rabbit pie, a famous specialty of the Acadians on Île Madame. Finally, everyone was ready: the twins had climbed back into the mailbag, the food was safely stowed away, and Johnny à Minou couldn't wait to leave.

Flabbergasted, Gabriel watched Johnny à Minou take a seven-league leap over Arichat cathedral while his two passengers sang:

We've got three strands of wool!
We've got three strands of wool!

It was cold among the stars, and the twins were glad to be snuggled inside Johnny à Minou's mailbag. They flew over the Strait of Canso, Havre Boucher, Tracadie,

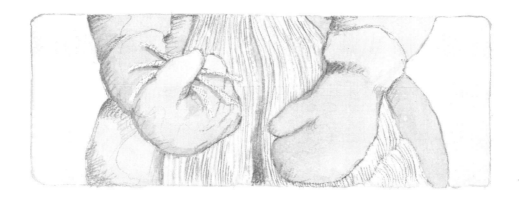

and dozens of ponds and inlets, but not a single one looked the slightest bit like a goose. Just when the three treasure hunters began to feel discouraged, they heard a familiar cry in the distance.

"Wild geese! Wild geese!" the twins exclaimed in unison.

"It must be the very last flock of the season," said Johnny à Minou. "Let's follow them. It's our only chance."

After flying for some time along the coast, the geese slowed down to land on a sheltered pond. Every year, hundreds of wild geese stopped there to rest and gather their strength for their journey south. Like a bird in flight, the pond stretched its blue wings over the snow-covered fields and meadows.

"It must be Goose Pond," said Rose-Marie.

"We can ask at the farmhouse over there," replied Constant.

Johnny à Minou started his descent, and they landed in the farmyard. To their amazement, the owner of the farm was expecting them. Just as she stepped out onto the porch to look at the star of Bethlehem, she saw the three travellers arrive. She approached them with both fear and curiosity. After they had all introduced themselves, the twins realized that the woman was the only living descendant of the shepherdess and that she too was called Thérésa. They also discovered that the village they had seen before they landed was Pomquet, on St. Georges Bay.

Convinced now that they were on the right track, Rose-Marie turned to Constant and said, "Show her the rug, show her Grannie Henriette's rug."

As soon as she saw the rug, Thérésa invited them in. Like everyone else, she was busy getting ready for Christmas, and the house was full of wonderful aromas. Thérésa was bursting with curiosity and listened attentively while Constant spoke.

"Grannie Henriette told us the story of the rug from Grand-Pré, and we're looking for some missing strands of wool. She would be so happy if we could find them."

"Oh! What good children you are. I think I can help. I know where you can find three more strands. Come out to the barn with me."

As Constant, Rose-Marie, and Johnny à Minou followed Thérésa outside, she explained to them that they were about to see one of the miracles of Christmas.

As every Acadian knows, no one is supposed to visit a stable on Christmas Eve, because the animals have magic powers on that night and can talk with each other. Whoever hears them speak will die within a year. But Thérésa, who had many a trick up her sleeve, knew how to protect the visitors. She handed them tiny balls of wax and told them to plug their left ears. That was the only way they could escape the evil spell. The right ear was out of harm's way.

Sure enough, the party was in full swing when they entered the barn. Cows, calves, ducks, hens, pigs, and sheep were chattering away.

Needless to say, Constant, Rose-Marie, and Johnny à Minou could hardly believe their right ears. All the animals were babbling away, except for two sheep off in a corner. They seemed very busy and were whispering in hushed tones.

Johnny à Minou and Rose-Marie were so enthralled that they completely forgot why they were there. Constant, who had wandered off on his own, overheard what the two sheep were saying.

"Do you really believe in the legend of the rug from Grand-Pré?" asked one sheep.

"Perhaps," replied the other. "If the legend is true, the wool seekers could be here any minute. And if we want to carry on the Christmas tradition as we have since the Deportation, we must start spinning right away."

With that, the two sheep began spinning three strands of wool. With her tail wagging, one helped the other by holding the wool in her teeth.

Meanwhile, all the other animals in the barn were busy laughing and talking. Rose-Marie, Thérésa, and Johnny à Minou forgot all about Constant.

"Tell me, ladies," Constant asked the sheep, "why do you spin three strands of wool every Christmas Eve?"

"Why, it's a tradition," they replied indignantly. "And who are you, young man?"

"My name is Constant, and I need some strands of wool. As a matter of fact, I need nine strands of wool to finish Grannie Henriette's hooked rug."

"A rug, did you say? And nine strands of wool? No, these strands of wool are not for you," said one of the sheep. "You see, we only spin three strands. We are waiting for twins to arrive with three other strands of wool from the fleece of one of our ancestors. Only then can we stop spinning on Christmas Eve."

Rose-Marie was the first to notice that Constant had gone off on his own. She was just about to go over to the sheep pen to get him when he beckoned to her.

"Rose-Marie! Come here! I think I've found the other strands of wool."

"Excuse me, young man," said one of the sheep, "we only spin three strands of wool, and even if that young lady is your twin sister, you have to prove that you have at least three strands of our ancestor's wool."

"That's easy," replied Constant. "Rose-Marie, show them the three strands Gabriel gave us, and if that's not proof enough, there are thousands more in Grannie Henriette's hooked rug."

Johnny à Minou pricked up his right ear and came over as the two sheep carefully examined the three strands that Rose-Marie took out of her pocket and placed at their feet.

"Those three strands definitely come from our ancestor's fleece," said one of the sheep. "I recognize the wool. But you also mentioned a rug, Grannie Henriette's rug. Can we see it?"

"Of course, here it is," Johnny à Minou replied as he held it up.

"The rug from Grand-Pré!" gasped the two sheep in one breath. "So the legend *is* true."

"This is what I wanted to show you, children," said Thérésa. "Ever since I was a little girl, there have always been two sheep in the flock who spin three strands of wool on Christmas Eve. My grandmother told me that the same thing happened during her lifetime. She said that according to the legend, the spell would be broken when the rug was finished."

"Here you are," said one of the sheep. "I'm sure these are the three strands you're looking for."

Rose-Marie clasped the six strands of wool tightly in her hand before putting them into her pocket. "What do we do now that we have six strands?" she immediately asked Johnny à Minou.

"I remember," added Thérésa, "that my grandmother also told me about a Captain Broussard who saved them from the British and took them to Pomquet. If I'm not mistaken, on one of his trips

Captain Broussard dropped anchor at a village called Pombcoup in the south of Acadie, on the molasses route. He spent Christmas there several times. He stayed with a family who lived in a large two-storey house across from the church, not far from the Pombcoup wharf. This family has always claimed to have the secret of the famous rug from Grand-Pré. You must go to Pombcoup, Johnny, to Céleste's house. You might find the missing strands there."

In a flash, the twins jumped back into the big mailbag, singing,

We've got three strands of wool!
We've got three strands of wool!

Thérésa made sure they were bundled up nicely. Then she gave them a deep-red blood pudding hot off the stove.

"Bon voyage! And good luck!"

Johnny à Minou took two or three running jumps and leaped over Goose Pond, leaving Pomquet behind. He quickly took his bearings and headed south. In three leaps and a bound, they were flying over the middle of Nova Scotia. In this part of Acadie, fir trees stretched out as far as the eye could see. From time to time, a frozen lake winked up at them from the land of the Christmas tree. The wind whistled past their ears, and the stars sparkled silently in the cold night.

"Johnny, what's that red star that seems to be coming toward us?"

Johnny à Minou quickened his step without saying a word. They could hear sleigh bells jingling as the star came closer.

"Constant! It's Santa Claus!" Rose-Marie cried out.

Forgetting his hunger for a moment and the blood pudding he was eating, Constant looked up just in time to see a sleigh flash by, drawn by nine reindeer, one with a shiny red nose.

"You'd better not look," Johnny à Minou said sternly as he smiled to himself. "I think we have just seen Santa Claus. He's in a hurry too."

As Johnny à Minou slipped past the stars, he took out his big mailman's watch and discovered that it was already nine-thirty. "We'll have to hurry if we are going to give Grannie Henriette the finished rug for Christmas." He led the twins over rivers and lakes, hills and barrens, until they finally saw the cross of a church steeple appear over the horizon.

On this Christmas Eve in Pombcoup—or Pubnico, as it is called today—the streets were bustling with activity. People and sleighs were coming and going. Chimneys were puffing their smoke into the still air. And sure enough, just as Thérésa had said, not far from the church was a large two-storey house, decorated for Christmas.

Céleste was so surprised to see a mailman that she threw open the door and said, "You must have a very urgent letter to come here on Christmas Eve."

"It's not a letter that brings me," said Johnny à Minou. "It's Grannie Henriette's twins."

"What do you mean, Grannie Henriette's twins?"

"Constant and Rose-Marie want to ask you something."

Without waiting another second, the twins climbed out of the mailbag and jumped onto the porch.

"Talk about a letter!" Céleste said, laughing. "Did you put a stamp on their bottoms so you could carry them in your Royal mailbag?"

"Excuse me," asked Rose-Marie, "is this where Captain Broussard spent Christmas in the olden days?"

"Yes, Captain Broussard spent Christmas with our family several times. Why do you ask?"

"I think you'll understand if I tell you we've come about the rug from Grand-Pré," Johnny à Minou added quickly.

"Have you found the rug from Grand-Pré? Come in, come in, children. Show me the rug right away. Our family has been waiting for this for a long time."

Filled with admiration, Céleste carefully examined the rug. Without saying a word, she went over to the antique wardrobe and slowly opened the bottom drawer. And there, as if waiting to be found, lay a yellowed envelope on which was written *Grand-Pré 1755.*

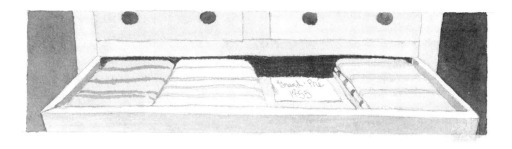

Céleste went back into the kitchen and placed the precious document in front of the twins.

"Children," she said, "this has been in our family ever since the unhappy years of the Deportation. We, the eldest daughters in the family, have handed this envelope down from one generation to the next, hoping that one day the guardians of the rug would come for it."

It was obvious from the expression on their faces that the children wanted to open the envelope immediately. Because Johnny à Minou knew all about letters, he opened the mysterious envelope very carefully with his little knife. Inside, there were three strands of wool. The twins jumped for joy.

We've got three strands of wool!
We've got three strands of wool!

They now had nine strands; they had to get only three more. At that moment, Céleste picked up the envelope and took out a note that added a whole new set of clues: *You will find three strands of bright red wool on the back of a holy lamb. When you have found all twelve strands of wool, you must hook them into the rug before Midnight Mass. Our ancestors are counting on you so that they can finally celebrate Christmas.*

"How are we ever going to find a holy lamb on Christmas Eve?" asked Constant, almost in tears. "A holy lamb that is bright red?"

"It's not midnight yet," replied Johnny à Minou, "and I'm sure that Céleste can help us."

The twins looked up at her hopefully.

"Well, children, so far you have found the wool in different parts of Acadie. You started in Chéticamp, then you went to Île Madame, from there you went to Pomquet, and then you came here to Pombcoup. You still haven't been to Baie Sainte Marie. I have a very good friend there who knows everything that goes on. Take this note, go see her, and tell her I sent you. Her name is Lucille, and she lives in a little house in La Butte."

That was just the clue the twins needed to continue their quest. Of course Céleste wouldn't think of letting them leave without a little something to nibble on. A little something in Pombcoup meant a big rappie pie and a double loaf of bread. Johnny à Minou's mailbag was beginning to look more and more like an enormous bag of groceries.

The twins couldn't wait to be on their way and tugged impatiently at Johnny à Minou. "Hold on, children, we're off," he cried.

No sooner said than done. In three strides, the twins and Johnny à Minou were up and away, leaving Céleste on her doorstep. The travellers were now racing among the stars as Wedgeport, Buttes Amirault, and Sainte Anne du Ruisseau swept by. They flew higher and higher into the sky. In the distance, they could see Rivière aux Saumons, Cap Sainte Marie, Saint Alphonse, Meteghan and, finally, La Butte.

"Are you sure we're on the right road, Johnny?" asked Rose-Marie.

"What! Don't you trust your favorite mailman any more?" laughed Johnny à Minou.

"Go faster, or we'll be late for Midnight Mass," said Constant.

Sure that his magic legs would not let him down on Christmas Eve, Johnny à Minou replied happily, "Don't worry, children, we're headed straight for La Butte, and we'll be there in time for Midnight Mass, my word of honor."

It was well past eleven o'clock when Johnny à
Minou began his descent toward La Butte. From high
in the sky, he had spotted Lucille's house. He landed
softly on her doorstep. Without even knocking, the
twins ran into the house and suddenly found
themselves in Lucille's arms.

"And who are you?"

"It's Constant and Rose-Marie, Grannie Henriette's twins," Johnny à Minou replied immediately. "Go ahead, children, show Lucille the note Céleste gave you. Then she'll understand everything."

"We have the rug too. Would you like to see it?"

"We haven't got time," Lucille said after reading the note quickly. "We must hurry. Johnny, take us right away to the church in La Pointe de l'Église before Midnight Mass begins. Here, children, take this pot of big clams in case you're hungry on your way back to Chéticamp."

Even with an extra passenger, Johnny à Minou moved quickly. In a wink, he was travelling at top speed toward La Pointe de l'Église.

Just imagine the surprise when Johnny à Minou, Lucille, and the twins landed right in the middle of all the people arriving for Midnight Mass. Without a second to spare, Johnny à Minou and the twins followed Lucille, who hurried to the sacristy, where Father Sigogne, dressed in his finest robes, was getting ready to say Mass.

"Father, I have something very important to ask you," Lucille said immediately. "Have you blessed a lamb recently?"

"But, my dear Lucille, you know perfectly well that I only bless lambs in the spring."

"This lamb would be easy to recognize," continued Lucille. "It's bright red."

"Bright red. Come now, Lucille, you know there is no such thing as a red lamb."

After hearing those words, Lucille and the twins did not know what to do next. The minutes were ticking by, and they absolutely had to find the strands of wool before midnight.

"No, I don't think I can help you. I must go. I have to say Midnight Mass. Come and see me in the presbytery, and we'll talk about it later."

Father Sigogne turned to go into the sanctuary, leaving the discouraged twins behind. Everything seemed hopeless. The last person who could help had just turned his back on them.

Suddenly, Lucille called out, "Stop, Father! Stop!"

Before Father Sigogne could turn around, Lucille rushed up with a pair of scissors to the gold cross on the back of his white chasuble. And there, in the centre of the cross, before their very eyes, was a lamb with a heart made of three bright-red strands of wool.

"Be careful, Lucille! You will ruin my beautiful chasuble. It dates back to the olden days. You know perfectly well that it is one of the parish treasures."

"It is for that very reason that the people of Grand-Pré could not have chosen a better place to hide the last strands of wool for the rug," Lucille replied, cutting off the three strands.

"My dear Lucille, have you found the hooked rug from Grand-Pré?" asked Father Sigogne.

"I didn't, Father, Grannie Henriette's twins did. We haven't a minute to spare. Johnny, you bring the rug, and you, children, you must finish hooking the rug before Mass begins."

St. Mary's church was packed, as it is every year. Constant and Rose-Marie spread the rug out on their knees and began to hook the twelve strands of wool they had found in the four corners of Acadie. On the

twelfth stroke of midnight, just as Mass was about to start, they finished hooking the twelfth and final strand.

"Look, Constant, Grannie Henriette's rug is finished," Rose-Marie whispered, bursting with joy.

The twins and Johnny à Minou happily admired the little cross on the steeple, finally able to see the result of all their efforts.

At that very moment, as if in a dream, they entered the magical world of their ancestors. A cloud of mist filled the church in La Pointe de l'Église and transported them to the church in Grand-Pré. Instead of being among villagers from Baie Sainte Marie, they were suddenly surrounded by Acadians of 1755.

"You must be Constant and Rose-Marie the twins. We've been waiting almost a century and a half for you so that we could celebrate our Christmas of 1755."

As their ancestors took the rug from Constant and Rose-Marie in order to hang it below the crucifix in the nave, the whole church was filled with light and the celebrations began.

The church turned into an enormous dance hall. No sooner had the pews been pushed back, tables set up, fiddles and guitars brought out, than their ancestors began to dance to lively tunes. Johnny à Minou opened his mailbag and poured onto the tables dozens of deep-red blood puddings, rappie pies, rabbit pies, and apple pies, pots of big clams, jugs of spruce beer, and double loaves of bread. At long last, their ancestors could celebrate the Christmas of 1755 right in front of Rose-Marie's and Constant's astonished eyes.

Suddenly, amid shouts of glee and laughter, a voice could be heard through the music: "Rose-Marie! Constant! Rose-Marie! Constant!"

Rose-Marie and Constant rubbed their eyes, trying to understand what was happening.

"Get up! Come and see!" Grannie Henriette called joyfully.

With that, the twins jumped out of bed and rushed downstairs to the Christmas tree. As they ran past the woodstove, they suddenly stopped and stared at the rug from Grand-Pré. All twelve strands of wool were there, in the cross on the steeple! The rug was finished!

The children stood spellbound. Grannie Henriette leaned over and whispered lovingly, "Thank you,

Constant and Rose-Marie, this is the happiest Christmas of my life."

The twins hugged Grannie Henriette and told her all about their adventures with Johnny à Minou.

What a miracle! The children had finished the rug, the most beautiful present they could ever give their grandmother and their ancestors. It was truly a magic rug.

If by chance you are in Grand-Pré at midnight on Christmas Eve, be sure to look carefully at the little church. If you see lights and if you hear the sounds of fiddles, guitars, and mandolins, you will know that our ancestors have come to celebrate Christmas—as they have done ever since Rose-Marie and Constant hooked the last strands of wool into the rug from Grand-Pré.

Nimbus Publishing Limited
P.O. Box 9301, Station A
Halifax, N.S.
B3K 5N5

Design and layout: Kathy Kaulbach
Illustrations: Copyright © by Herménégilde Chiasson
Hooked rug: Henriette Aucoin

Photograph of Herménégilde Chiasson: Dolorès Breau/courtesy NSCAD

Canadian Cataloguing in Publication Data

Aucoin, Réjean, 1955–

Tapis de Grand-Pré. English.

The magic rug of Grand-Pré

Translation of: Le tapis de Grand-Pré.
ISBN 0-921054-20-3

I. Tremblay, Jean-Claude. II. Chiasson, Herménégilde, 1946– III. Title.
IV. Title: Tapis de Grand-Pré. English.

PS8551.U26T313 1989   jC843'.54   C89-098625-8   PZ7.A92Ma 1989

Printed and bound in Canada